W9-BMJ-654

Hot Rod Hamster and the Haunted Halloween Party!

By Cynthia Lord
Cover illustration by Derek Anderson
Interior illustrations by Greg Paprocki

SCHOLASTIC INC.

To Emily. — C. L.

For my grandparents, Walter and Margaret Schwab, who always had treats! — D. A.

Text copyright © 2015 by Cynthia Lord
Illustrations copyright © 2015 by Derek Anderson
This book is being published simultaneously in hardcover by Scholastic Press.
All rights reserved. Published by Scholastic Inc., *Publishers since 1920*. SCHOLASTIC, SCHOLASTIC PRESS, and associated logos are trademarks and/or registered trademarks of Scholastic Inc.
The publisher does not have any control over and does not assume any responsibility for author or third-party websites or their content.
No part of this publication may be reproduced, stored in a retrieval system, or transmitted in any form or by any means, electronic, mechanical, photocopying, recording, or otherwise, without written permission of the publisher. For information regarding permission, write to Scholastic Inc., Attention: Permissions Department, 557 Broadway, New York, NY 10012.

LIBRARY OF CONGRESS CATALOGING-IN-PUBLICATION DATA
Lord, Cynthia, author.
Hot Rod Hamster and the haunted Halloween party / by Cynthia Lord ; cover illustration by Derek Anderson ; interior illustrations by Greg Paprocki. — First edition. pages cm
Summary: Hot Rod Hamster is invited to a Halloween party, and he enlists the help of a group of ghosts to win the spookiest costume contest.
ISBN 978-0-545-81528-4
1. Hamsters—Juvenile fiction. 2. Halloween costumes—Juvenile fiction. 3. Halloween—Juvenile fiction. 4. Contests—Juvenile fiction. 5. Parties—Juvenile fiction. [1. Hamsters—Fiction. 2. Costume—Fiction. 3. Ghosts—Fiction. 4. Halloween—Fiction. 5. Contests—Fiction. 6. Parties—Fiction.] I. Anderson, Derek, 1969–illustrator. II. Paprocki, Greg, illustrator. III. Title. PZ7.L87734Houk 2015 813.6—dc23 [E] 2014038852

10 9 8 7 6 5 4 3 2 15 16 17 18 19/0

Printed in Malaysia 108
First printing 2015

The display type was set in Ziggy ITC and Coop Black.
The text was set in Cochin Medium and Gill Sans Bold.
The interior art was created digitally by Greg Paprocki.
Art direction and book design by Marijka Kostiw

It was Halloween. Hot Rod Hamster hurried off to find his friend Dog. He was on the run to show Dog something fun.

Dog, look what came in the mail!
It's a Halloween party! There will be prizes, games, food, and fun! Let's go!
WHAT?
Halloween Party
WHEN?
October 31. From 5 to 8 p.m.
WHERE?
The town square
WHO?
YOU! Bring your friends, too.
Prizes for the best and the spookiest costumes!
FUN! GAMES! FRIGHTFULLY GOOD FOOD!

Okay! We'll need some costumes. We must go to the store.

Ghost fun. Clown fun.
Star fun. Crown fun.
SALE

Which would *you* choose?

I want to be a rock star!
And we can be your band! We should have some instruments.
RIP

Which would *you* choose?

I'm ready to rock and roll! Maybe we'll win the prize for best costume!

We will look great, but a rock band needs a stage to perform on.

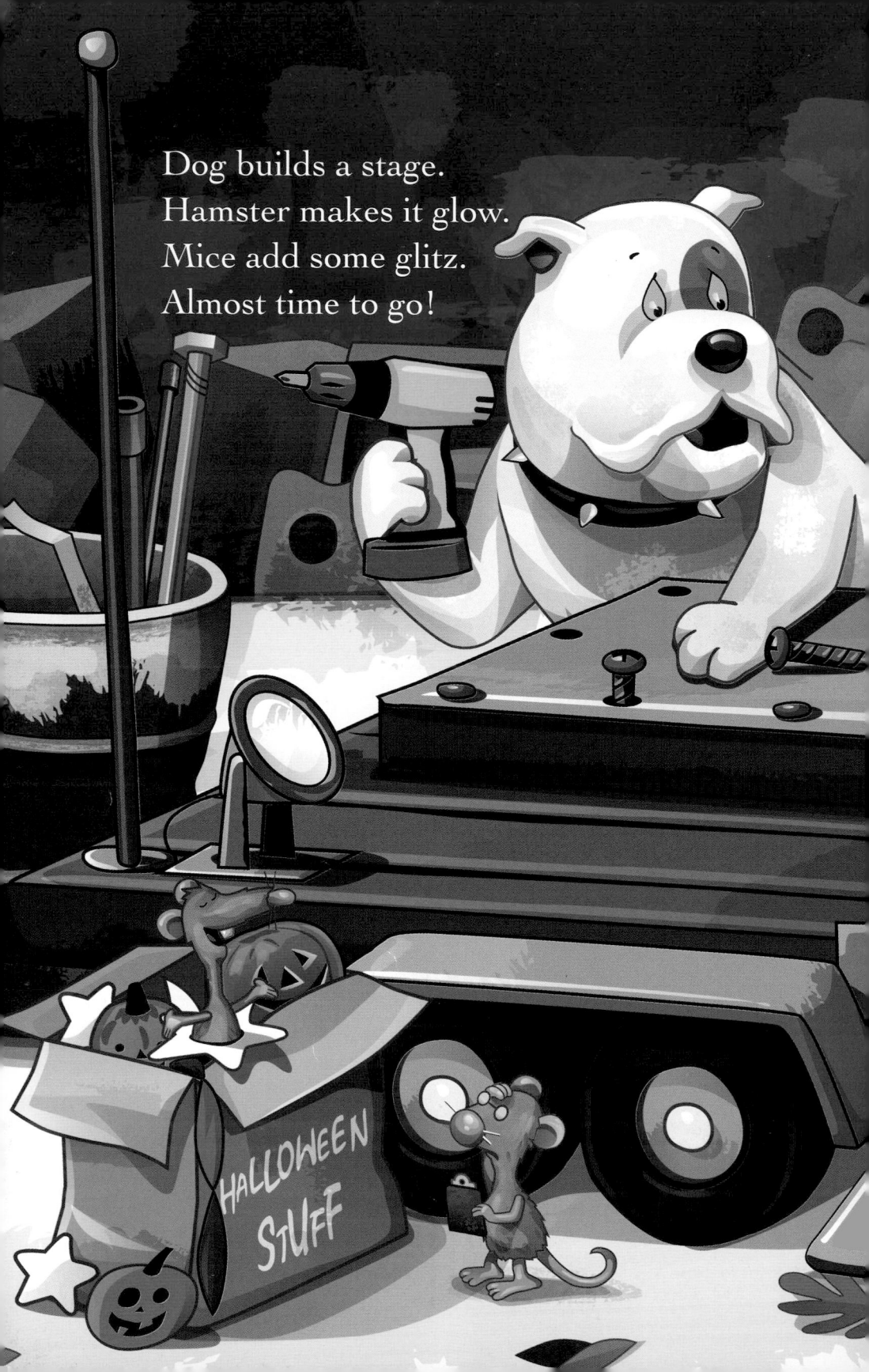
Dog builds a stage.
Hamster makes it glow.
Mice add some glitz.
Almost time to go!
HALLOWEEN
STUFF

Now we need
a spooky song to sing.
Halloween is fun and spooky, too!
What rhymes
with "too"?

Hmm, what rhymes with "too"? Blue? Shoe?

Dog tries to help Hamster with his song.
Mice dream of fun, but—oh no!
Something's wrong.

I'm sorry. The hot rod has broken down. I could fix it if I had some tools.
It's almost time for the party. Let's ask for help at this house.

Dog isn't sure, but Hamster steps inside . . .

Mice stop and gasp. Their eyes open wide.

Ooooh, a party?
I love parties!
Does the party have treats? And music?
If we loan you the tools, can we come to the party, too?
I have a great idea!

Such a spooky place!
I feel right at home!

Welcome to the Halloween party!

Carve time?

Which would *you* choose?

Dog carves pumpkins.
Hamster tastes the brew.

Ghosts float around and practice saying "Boo!"
RIP
Boo!
HELLO MY NAME IS
HELLO MY NAME IS
It's time for the costume judging!
Everyone get ready!

Dog taps the beat.
Hamster counts a few.
Here we go! One, two, three, four!

Mice take their spots,
backup singers, too.

Dog plays the drums.
Hamster sings his song.
Mice shake and dance.
The ghosts howl along.
Halloween is fun and spooky, too! Black cats, spiders, and ghosts say—

Booooooo0000ooooo!
The winner for the best AND the spookiest costume —

Hot Rod Hamster and His Howl-Agains!
Thank you! HAPPY HALLOWEEN, EVERYONE!